April, 2003
Easter

*T*his book belongs to

Liam

THE DOVE AWARD SIGNATURE SERIES

I've Just Seen Jesus

A VERY SPECIAL STORY FOR CHILDREN

BASED ON THE DOVE AWARD™ SONG SUNG BY *Larnelle Harris*

STORY WRITTEN BY STEPHEN ELKINS · NARRATED BY LARNELLE HARRIS

ILLUSTRATED BY ELLIE COLTON

BROADMAN
& HOLMAN
PUBLISHERS

Nashville, Tennessee

With special thanks to Frank Breeden, Bonnie Pritchard, and the Gospel Music Association.

Song performed by the Wonder Kids Choir:
Emily Elkins, Laurie Evans, Amy Lawrence, Lindsay McAdams,
Amy McPeak, and Olivia Evans
Solo performed by Emily Elkins.

Arranged and produced by Stephen Elkins.
CD recorded in a split-track format.
Recorded at Wonder Workshop, Mt. Juliet, TN

Published in 2003 by Broadman & Holman Publishers, Nashville, Tennessee

Cover layout by Deann Hebert.
Interior layout by Ed Maksimowicz.

DEWEY: C781.7
SUBHD: JESUS CHRIST \ POPULAR CHRISTIAN MUSIC--TEXTS

ISBN 0-8054-2665-5

1 2 3 4 5   07 06 05 04 03

This book is dedicated to my ministry family at Broadman & Holman Publishers, whose commitment to children's ministry facilitates these kinds of Christian education tools that we pray may enable a child to "see Jesus." I say thank you for all that you are doing.

Hebrews 6:10

We knew He was dead. "It is finished," He said. We watched as His life ebbed away.

For a moment, we forgot we were watching an Easter play. We were swept away to another time and another place as the Easter story came to life right before our eyes.

As the curtain slowly fell, Jesus, played by my best friend Jason, looked to heaven and spoke, "Father, into your hands I commit my spirit." He bowed His head and died.

Then we all stood around, 'til the guards took Him down.

When the curtain rose again every eye was fixed on the character of Jesus. It was as if the entire congregation could feel the suffering Jesus endured on the cross that first Easter.

As the Roman guards prepared to remove Jesus' body, two well-dressed men appeared on the stage. "I am Joseph, a friend of Jesus," one of them said to the guards. "May I have the body, so that I may give Jesus a proper burial?"

"No," said the gruff centurion. "Go away! His body is the property of Rome."

9

Joseph begged for His body that day.

He knew Jesus was the Son of God and wanted Him to have an honorable burial. So, at great risk, he pleaded, "Sirs, I beg of you. I have spoken to Pilate and he assured me I could have the body. Please … He was my friend."

"Take the body," growled the guard.

"Who would want the body of a convicted criminal anyway?" But Joseph knew Jesus had done no wrong. He was crucified for who He was, the Son of God.

So Nicodemus and Joseph carried Jesus away as the curtain fell again.

As the next act began, a young woman named Mary Magdalene, played by my sister Susan, was pleading with the disciples to come with her.

It was late afternoon; and we went down to the tomb, left His body, and sealed up the grave.

Mary continued, "We planned to visit the tomb where Jesus was buried, but when we arrived, we saw something miraculous!"

Peter spoke up, "Miraculous? Our Messiah is dead and you speak of miracles?"

"The giant stone had been rolled away and Jesus was gone!" Mary exclaimed.

"Gone? Where?" Peter asked angrily.

"Who would take His body? John, come with me. Let us see for ourselves!" Peter and John quickly ran off the stage.

Mary continued to plead with the other disciples.

Oh, I know how you feel; His death was so real. But, please listen, and hear what I say.

I'VE JUST SEEN JESUS

"Not only was His body gone, but there was an angel at the tomb," Mary explained.

"Angel?" scoffed Thomas.

"He was real, I tell you. And he told me, 'Jesus is not here, He is alive!' Then I met a gardener who asked me why I was crying. I told him that my Lord had been crucified, and that His body had been taken. Then He spoke my name. 'Mary,' He said. And I knew it was Jesus!"

"It was who?" asked Thomas.

"It was Jesus! He has risen!" Mary said.

I've just seen Jesus!
I tell you He's alive!

I'VE JUST SEEN JESUS

"Alive?" said James. "We saw Him crucified by Roman soldiers. We saw the nails pierce His hands and feet. We saw the blood."

"We saw Jesus die!" Andrew interrupted. "He is dead and nothing can change that."

"A miracle could change that," spoke Mary. "He made the blind to see, the lame to walk. James, you saw Him walk on the water."

I've just seen Jesus, our precious Lord, alive.

"Maybe you're right Mary," James said hopefully. "Andrew, what was it He told us before He died?"

"Destroy this temple and I will build it again in three days," quoted Andrew.

"How long since He died?" asked James.

"Three days!" exclaimed Mary. "Three days … He's alive, and I saw Him!"

And I knew He really saw me too. As if 'til now I've never lived.

I'VE JUST SEEN JESUS

"You saw Him with your own eyes?" asked Thomas.

"Yes," said Mary. "And with His smile He said, 'I love you and everything is going to be alright.' I knew He had saved me. I knew I was free."

All that I've done before, won't matter anymore.

I'VE JUST SEEN JESUS

"He washed my sins away and I am a new creation. Oh, you must come and see Him!"

Thomas raised his voice and said, "I will not believe until I touch His nail-pierced hands and side."

At that moment Peter and John burst into the room. "He is risen," exclaimed John. "Our Lord has risen! We've been to the tomb and it is empty; only the grave clothes remain." Hope filled the room. The disciples began to recall the words of Jesus as Simon and Cleopas entered.

I've just seen Jesus, and I'll never be the same again!

I'VE JUST SEEN JESUS

These were the words of Cleopas who had seen the risen Jesus that day on the road to Emmaus. As he spoke to the disciples, Jesus appeared before them and said, "Peace be with you. Why are you troubled and why do you doubt?" He showed them His nail-pierced hands.

When Thomas saw the scars on Jesus' hands and feet, he believed. Jesus said to him, "Because you have seen you have believed. Blessed are those who have not seen and believe."

The play ended and the curtain closed. Pastor Morgan stepped forward to speak to the audience.

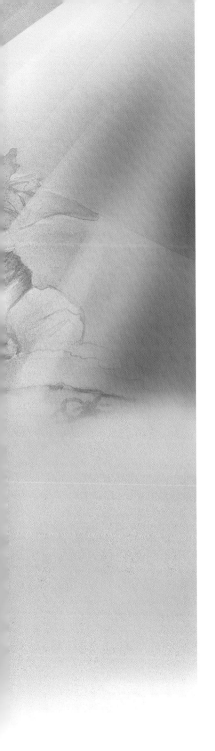

It was His voice she first heard, those kind gentle words, asking what was her reason for tears.

I'VE JUST SEEN JESUS

Mary was crying because she thought all was lost. Her hope was gone. Her Savior was dead. But we know Jesus lives today.

"After His resurrection, Jesus appeared many times," Pastor Morgan said. "Often, just to comfort one person, like Mary."

And I sobbed in despair, "My Lord is not there!" He said, "It is I, I am here."

Mary saw Jesus. Cleopas and Simon saw Jesus. He appeared to the eleven disciples as they gathered in the room where they had all been together for the last time. He appeared to over five hundred people before returning to His Father in heaven.

And Jesus sits at the right hand of the Father until His return. But remember His words to Thomas, "Blessed are those who have not seen and yet believe."

Then Pastor Morgan proclaimed. . .

I've just seen Jesus!
I tell you He's alive!
I've just seen Jesus, our
precious Lord alive.

We won't see Jesus with our eyes until He returns again, but by faith we believe and know He lives.

As the players came back on to the stage, we all bowed our heads to pray. It was an Easter none of us would ever forget. It was as if we had seen Jesus . . . and we'll never be the same again!

Don't miss the other titles in the Dove Award™ Signature Series for Children

The Great Adventure
Based on the Dove Award™ Song
by Steven Curtis Chapman

0-8054-2399-0

Thank You
Based on the Dove Award™ Song
by Ray Boltz

0-8054-2400-8

God is In Control
Based on the Dove Award™ Song
by Twila Paris

0-8054-2402-4

Testify to Love
Based on the Dove Award™ Song
by Avalon

0-8054-2416-4

Awesome God
Based on the Dove Award™ Song
by Rich Mullins

0-8054-2664-7

Available at Christian Bookstores everywhere.